nature's friends

Fireflies

by Ann Heinrichs

Science Adviser: Terrence E. Young Jr., M.Ed., M.L.S., Jefferson Parish (La.) Public Schools
Content Adviser: Jan Jenner, Ph.D.
Reading Adviser: Dr. Linda D. Labbo, Department of Reading Education, College of Education, The University of Georgia

COMPASS POINT BOOKS
MINNEAPOLIS, MINNESOTA

Compass Point Books
3109 West 50th Street, #115
Minneapolis, MN 55410

Visit Compass Point Books on the Internet at *www.compasspointbooks.com*
or e-mail your request to *custserv@compasspointbooks.com*

Photographs ©: Dwight Kuhn, cover, 10–11, 12–13; Bruce Coleman Inc./E. R. Degginger, 4–5; Bruce Coleman Inc./John M. Burnley, 7, 18–19; J. E. Lloyd U.F., 8, 15, 23, 26–27; Bruce Coleman Inc./Ivan Polunin, 16–17; Bill Beatty, 20–21; Robert A. Flynn, 24–25.

Editor: Patricia Stockland
Photo Researcher: Marcie C. Spence
Designer: The Design Lab

Library of Congress Cataloging-in-Publication Data
Heinrichs, Ann.
  Fireflies / by Ann Heinrichs.
  p. cm. — (Nature's friends)
Summary: Describes different types of fireflies and their physical characteristics, how and why they light up, their uses to mankind, and their life cycles.
Includes bibliographical references and index (p.   ).
ISBN 0-7565-0588-7 (hardcover)
1. Fireflies—Juvenile literature. [1. Fireflies.] I. Title. II. Series.
QL596.L28H45 2004
595.76'44—dc22   2003014434

© 2004 by Compass Point Books
All rights reserved. No part of this book may be reproduced without written permission from the publisher. The publisher takes no responsibility for the use of any of the materials or methods described in this book, nor for the products thereof.
Printed in the United States of America.

Table of Contents

Nature's Magical Light Show 5

Fireflies Around the World 6

What Is a Firefly? 9

A Firefly's Body 10

How Do Fireflies Light Up? 13

Why Do They Light Up? 14

Are You My Species? 17

Mating and Laying Eggs 18

A Larva's Life 21

Becoming an Adult 22

Fireflies Helping the World 25

Fun with Firefly Friends 26

Glossary 28

Let's Look at Fireflies 29

Did You Know? 29

Junior Entomologists 30

Want to Know More? 31

Index 32

NOTE: In this book, words that are defined in the glossary are in **bold** *the first time they appear in the text.*

Nature's Magical Light Show

Like sparkles, glancing to and fro
Among the new-mown grass,
The fireflies gleam; how strange the show!
As back and forth they pass.
— *from "The Fireflies," by Jones Very (1870)*

Have you ever chased fireflies on a warm summer night? Maybe you call them lightning bugs or glowworms. Their tiny, floating sparks of light twinkle like stars.

Fireflies have always seemed magical to humans. A Japanese **myth** says they are the tears of the Moon Princess. A Native American **legend** says fireflies created fire. In ancient Mexico, a firefly was the Queen of Stars.

Now let's shed some light on our firefly friends!

◀ *You may have seen fireflies like these during the summer.*

Fireflies Around the World

People around the world love fireflies. Many Japanese villages even hold firefly festivals. Malaysia has a nature park just for fireflies.

Fireflies live on every continent except Antarctica. They like warm areas with water nearby. There are more than 1,900 species, or types, of fireflies around the world. Central and South America and tropical Asia have the most species.

Different species have different colors of lights. The lights may be yellow, white, green, orange, or yellowish-brown. Some species do not light up at all.

The *Photinus pyralis* is the best-known species in North America. Its nickname is the Big Dipper firefly. It is less than 1 inch (2.5 centimeters) long.

Photinus pyralis, *the Big Dipper firefly* ▶

What Is a Firefly?

Fireflies are insects. However, they are not flies. They are really beetles!

Scientists call beetles in the firefly family Lampyridae. That is a big word, but it's a good name for fireflies. It comes from the Greek words for "shining fire." Did you notice the word *lamp* is part of *Lampyridae,* too?

Fireflies are sometimes called soft-bodied beetles. A firefly has an exoskeleton on the outside of its body. The exoskeleton is like a shell. It protects the firefly's body. Most beetles have a hard exoskeleton. However, a firefly's exoskeleton is soft.

◀ *Fireflies are actually beetles.*

A Firefly's Body

Like all insects, a firefly has three main body parts. They are the head, thorax, and abdomen.

The head has two eyes and two antennae, or feelers. It also has mouthparts. These are parts near the mouth that the firefly uses for eating or gathering things. The thorax is the firefly's middle section. The front of the thorax is a hard plate. It covers the head like a roof. The abdomen is the firefly's end section. It contains parts for breathing and lighting up.

Fireflies have six legs. Most species have four wings. They extend down to the end of the body. The two inner wings are soft. The two outer wings are harder.

The back end, or abdomen, of this firefly is the part that lights up. ▶

How Do Fireflies Light Up?

Remember the firefly's abdomen? That is where the firefly breathes. It is also where it lights up.

When a firefly breathes, it takes in **oxygen.** The oxygen mixes with special **chemicals** inside the firefly—luciferin, luciferase, and adenosine triphosphate, or ATP. When this mixture happens, the abdomen lights up.

Have you ever touched a light bulb that was turned on? If you did, you probably found it was hot. Light bulbs send out a hot light. A firefly's light is a "cold light." It does not give off heat.

◀ *A firefly's light is not hot.*

Why Do They Light Up?

Why do fireflies light up? Mostly, they do it to find a mate.

The male flies around flashing his light. Meanwhile, the female is near the ground. She flashes an "answer." Then the male flies down to find her!

Flashing also protects a firefly from birds and other insects. The light tells them that fireflies are no good to eat! The firefly's chemicals taste really bad.

Fireflies can also flash a special **distress** signal. Suppose a firefly gets caught in a spider web. Its signal could mean "Help!" or "Stay away from here!" The distress signal warns other fireflies of the danger.

This firefly, Photinus pallens, *flashes while it is wrapped into the spider's web.* ▶

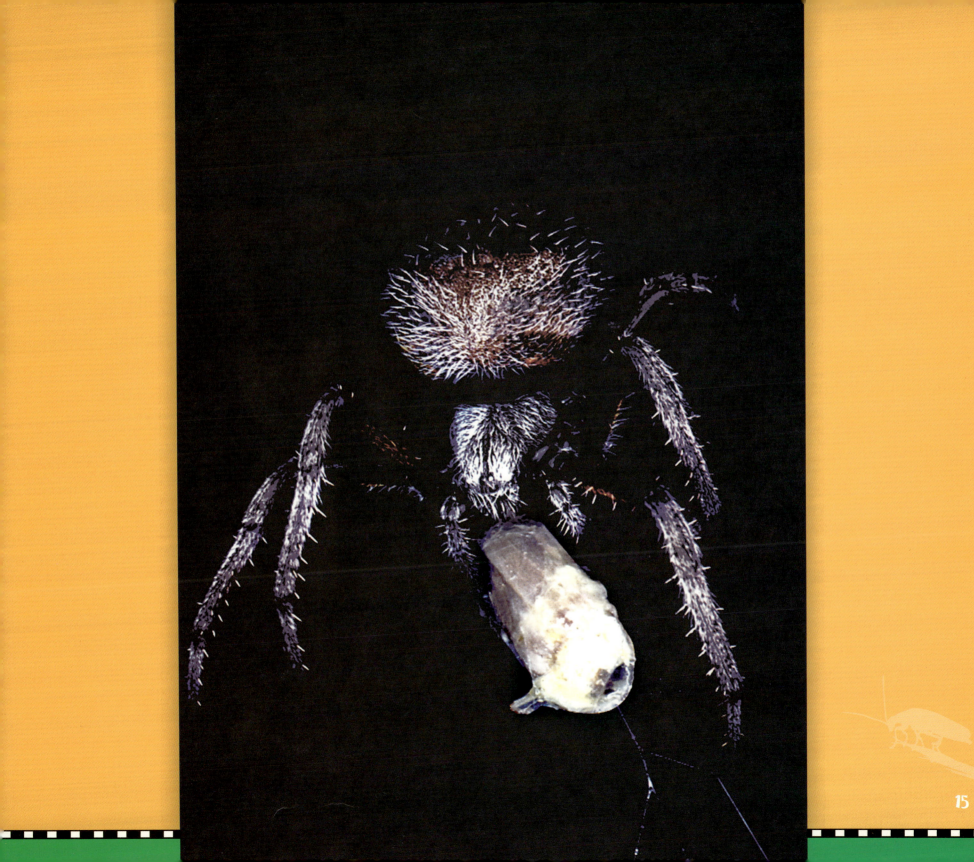

Are You My Species?

A firefly will only mate with its own species. Suppose you were a firefly. How would you find a firefly of your own species?

Each species has its own flashing pattern. Some make short, quick flashes. Some wait longer between flashes. Others keep their lights on longer. Some make many flashes in a row, called "flash-trains."

One Asian firefly species blinks along with its neighbors. Hundreds of fireflies gather in a tree. One begins its special flashing pattern. Then the others join in. Soon the whole tree is blinking on and off together!

◀ *A Malaysian firefly tree may have hundreds of fireflies blinking together.*

Mating and Laying Eggs

After a male and female find each other, they mate. Then the female is able to lay eggs. She lays them in a damp place. It could be wet soil, rotting wood, or dead leaves. Often it is near a stream or pond.

The female may lay 500 eggs or more. Even the eggs have a soft glow! In two to four weeks, the eggs hatch.

Photinus pyralis *fireflies mate on a leaf.* ▶

A Larva's Life

A firefly has three stages of life. They are the larva, pupa, and adult stages.

When a firefly egg hatches, out comes a larva. The larva looks like a tiny turtle or worm. It has lots of legs but no wings. In many species, the larva can light up. That larva is sometimes called a glowworm.

The larva eats earthworms, snails, and slugs. It injects **venom** into its **prey.** The venom turns the prey into a liquid. Then the larva can suck it in.

Life as a larva lasts one to two years.

◀ *A firefly larva attacks a slug.*

Becoming an Adult

One warm spring day, it is time for a change. It is time for the larva to become a pupa! As a pupa, the larva will develop the body parts of an adult.

In one species, the larva builds a little mud case the size of a marble. Then it climbs inside to become a pupa. In some species, the pupa hangs from a tree.

It is only a pupa for a short time. In about two weeks, the covering breaks open. Out comes an adult firefly.

Some adult fireflies eat **nectar** and **pollen** from flowers. Some eat other insects—or nothing at all! Some species live a few weeks or months as adults. Others live only a few days.

A pupa breaks open its larval case. Within hours, it will be ready to fly. ▸

Fireflies Helping the World

Fireflies may be small. Still, they do amazing things for humans.

A firefly's light-making chemicals are very useful. Doctors use them to study heart and muscle diseases. Scientists use them to test new drugs for deadly diseases. The chemicals can also detect air and water **pollution.** They are used to test foods and drinking water for safety.

Fireflies have a great future in the science world. Scientists say their chemicals can even detect life in outer space!

◀ *These scientists are studying the chemicals that make fireflies flash.*

Fun with Firefly Friends

Fireflies are good friends. They do not bite or sting. They are fun to watch, too.

Look for fireflies on a warm summer night. They like dark, grassy places the best. If outdoor lights are shining, they cannot see one another!

Watch for different blinking patterns. Then you can pick out different species. Watch for fireflies twinkling in the grass. They are females.

You can catch fireflies and put them in a jar. Handle them carefully. Make sure the jar has airholes. Watch them light up in a dark room. Then let them go again. After all, their lives are short. They have important work to do!

Fireflies are our friends. ▶

Glossary

chemicals—the basic substances that make up all materials

distress—a feeling of worry, danger, or pain

legend—a story that is popular but probably not true

myth—an old story that helps people understand the natural world

nectar—a sweet liquid matter that is produced by some plants

oxygen—a gas found in air

pollen—the tiny bits of dust from a plant that fertilize the seeds

pollution—waste that people put into the water, land, and air

prey—an animal hunted by another animal for food

venom—a liquid that some animals inject to stun or kill their prey

Let's Look at Fireflies

Class: Insecta
Order: Coleoptera
Family: Lampyridae
Species: There are more than 1,900 species of fireflies worldwide. About 175 species live in the United States.

Range: Fireflies live in all regions except the continent of Antarctica. The greatest numbers of fireflies are found in warm, moist climates.

Life stages: Female fireflies lay 500 or more eggs in damp places. Larvae hatch from the eggs. They cannot fly. Firefly larvae spend one to two years developing. Next comes the pupa stage. During that time, the firefly develops into an adult. This stage lasts 10 days to two weeks.

Life span: Adult fireflies live for five days to several months, depending on the species.

Food: Firefly larvae eat earthworms, snails, slugs, and other insects in the larval stages. Some adult fireflies eat the nectar and pollen of flowers. Some species eat other insects. Some eat nothing at all.

Did You Know?

Frogs eat fireflies. Sometimes frogs eat so many fireflies that their stomach area glows!

The common pyralis firefly is also called the Big Dipper firefly. The Big Dipper is a constellation, or pattern of stars in the sky.

Fireflies that glow are rarely seen in the western United States.

In some firefly species, the female imitates the flashing pattern of other species. When the male comes near, the female eats him!

Several animals are bioluminescent, or light-giving. They include jellyfish, certain fishes, and some tiny sea creatures.

The word *glowworm* is used to describe several insects. One is the wingless female of one firefly species. Another is the glowing firefly larva. A third glowworm is the phengodid, or click beetle.

Junior Entomologists

Entomologists are scientists who study insects. You can be an entomologist, too! Find a large, clean glass jar with a cover. You will also need an insect-catching net, a flashlight, a notebook, and a pencil. Have an adult help you poke some airholes in the cover of your jar. Then go outside when it starts getting dark, and look for fireflies. Some good places to look are in tall grass, at the edge of a wooded area, or by a stream. Gently capture at least five fireflies, and place them in your jar. Set the jar down. Observe the flashing lights in the jar for 10 minutes. Record your observations in your notebook. Next, use the light from your flashlight to get a better look at the fireflies. Write down your observations. Try to answer the questions below. Finally, take the jar back outside to the spot where you caught the fireflies. Open the jar, and let the fireflies fly away.

Now try to answer the following questions:

How many fireflies did you observe?

Did they all look the same? Were they the same color and size?

Did you notice any patterns to the flashes of light? Do you think the fireflies were all the same species?

Did all of the fireflies flash their lights at once, or did it look like they were "answering" each other's flashes?

Did the fireflies flash from the same height? Do you think some were male and some were female?

Draw a picture of a firefly.

Want to Know More?

AT THE LIBRARY
Brinckloe, Julie. *Fireflies!* New York: Aladdin Books, 1986.

Hawes, Judy, and Ellen Alexander (illustrator). *Fireflies in the Night.* New York: HarperCollins, 1991.

Johnson, Sylvia A., and Satoshi Kuribayashi (photographer). *Fireflies.* Minneapolis: Lerner, 1986.

ON THE WEB

For more information on **fireflies,** use FactHound to track down Web sites related to this book.

1. Go to www.compasspointbooks.com/facthound
2. Type in this book ID: **0756505887**
3. Click on the *Fetch It* button.

Your trusty FactHound will fetch the best Web sites for you!

THROUGH THE MAIL
National Museum of Natural History
O. Orkin Insect Zoo
Office of Education
Constitution Avenue and 10th Street N.W.
Washington, DC 20560
202/357-2700
For more information on the life and habits of fireflies

ON THE ROAD
Museum of Biological Diversity
Insect Collection
Ohio State University
1315 Kinnear Road
Columbus, OH 43212
614/292-7773
To see a collection of millions of insects, including fireflies

Montshire Museum of Science
One Montshire Road
Norwich, VT 05055
802/649-2200
To see nearly 20 species of fireflies and observe their different flashing patterns

Index

abdomen, 10, 13
adenosine triphosphate (ATP), 13
adult stage, 21, 22
antennae, 10

Big Dipper firefly. See Photinus pyralis.
breathing, 13

Central America, 6
chemicals, 13, 14, 25
"cold light," 13
color, 6

distress signals, 14
doctors, 25

eggs, 18
exoskeleton, 9
eyes, 10

feelers. See antennae.

"The Fireflies" (Jones Very), 5
fireflies, *4–5*, 7, *8*, *11*, *12–13*, *16–17*, 27
"flash-trains," 17
flashing patterns, 17, 26
food, 21, 22

glowworms, 5, 21

head, 10

Lampyridae family, 9
larva stage, *20*, 21–22
larval case, 22, *23*
legends, 5
legs, 10
life span, 22
lights, 6, 13–14, 17, 21
luciferase, 13
luciferin, 13

mating, 14, 17, 18, *19*

mouth, 10
myths, 5

nectar, 22

Photinus pallens, 15
Photinus pyralis, 6, 7, *19*
pollen, 22
pollution, 25
prey, 21
pupa stage, 21, 22, *23*

scientists, *24–25*, 25
slugs, *20–21*, 21
species, 6
spider webs, 14, *15*

thorax, 10

venom, 21
Very, Jones, 5

wings, 10

About the Author: Ann Heinrichs grew up in Fort Smith, Arkansas. She began playing the piano at age three and thought she would grow up to be a pianist. Instead, she became a writer. She has written more than 100 books for children and young adults. Several of her books have won national awards. Ms. Heinrichs now lives in Chicago, Illinois. She enjoys martial arts and traveling to faraway countries.